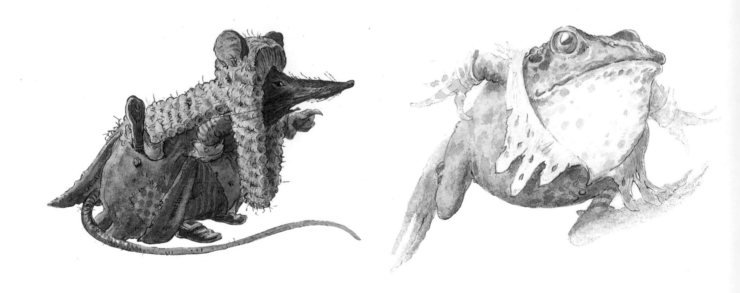

The Evergreen Wood

ALAN & LINDA PARRY

Hunt & Thorpe

ISBN 1 85608 145 1

In Australia this book is published by:
Hunt & Thorpe Australia Pty Ltd., 9 Euston Street,
Rydalmere NSW 2116.

A CIP catalogue record for this book is available
from the British Library.

Manufactured in Hong Kong.

Christopher's Journey

Swamp

The Dark Wood

The Great Oak Tree

The Steep Hill

Wildcat

The Black Valley

Rat Fair

Beak

Narrow Gate

N

Badger's House

Fox Territory

Cedar Grove

Enchanted Ground

The Glade

The Evergreen Wood

CHAPTER 1
THE DARK WOOD

Christopher Mouse looked around him. The Dark Wood, the place where he had always lived, was in poor shape.

The stream that used to sparkle with freshness had turned muddy brown, and bubbles foamed up on its banks. Most of the best trees had been cut down, and nobody had bothered to plant any more.

Strong winds now blew straight through the once dense wood. Much of the soft, loamy earth, which the mice made their homes in, had blown away, leaving the ground hard and barren.

Christopher sighed. "And what's more," he

mused, "owls and hawks are on the increase, and it's not so easy to hide from them these days."

Then, as he pondered these things, he came across a notice pinned on one of the trees:

Dark Wood–Sold
For Development
~
All creatures of this
wood are invited to
make the long journey
to The Evergreen Wood,
where they may live
in peace and safety.

There was a lot more writing, and Christopher read it all and saw that it was signed by the King of that country. He unpinned the notice from the tree and rushed home to show his wife and children.

"It says on this notice," he proclaimed, "that our wood is to be destroyed and that we may go to another place, a long way off, where we shall be safe!"

But his wife, Christina, was busy cooking, and the children were pretending to be pirates.

Mother said she certainly did not think it would happen in *her* lifetime. The children asked if there would be swords and spears to play with there. And when Father said, "Certainly not!" they

grumbled about it not being much fun. Besides, they hated walking.

However hard he tried, Christopher could not persuade any of his family or friends even to consider making the journey.

Christopher grew sadder and sadder. He seemed to be the only creature who believed the warning on the notice. The sadness became a great weight on his shoulders, and before long Christopher was carrying a heavy burden on his back.

He knew he must start the journey to The Evergreen Wood, but he did not know the way to go.

Then he saw a white mouse coming toward him. Christopher trembled a little. He remembered reading on the notice that there were many white mice in The Evergreen Wood. As the mouse came nearer, he smiled. He seemed to know Christopher!

"Why are you looking so sad, my friend?" he asked.

"Because I have read," replied Christopher, "on this notice, that The Dark Wood is to be destroyed and that its inhabitants can escape to another place, The Evergreen Wood. But," he sighed, "I do not know the way."

"Do you see that narrow gate in the distance?"

asked the White Mouse, pointing with his paw over a very wide field.

"I think I do," said Christopher, looking hard in that direction.

"Follow this path," said the mouse, "and you will reach it. Then you will be told the way."

"Thank you," called Christopher, who was already running towards the gate.

His wife and children saw him run off and yelled after him to come back. The other creatures, too, tried to make him return.

Two young rabbits, named Stickle and Fickle, chased after him. "Where are you going, Christopher?" they asked.

"To another place, where all creatures are protected—where the owls and hawks and foxes won't eat us," explained Christopher. "Everybody there lives together in peace."

The rabbits giggled. "Sounds like a fairy tale," laughed Stickle.

"It's true," said Christopher. "Why don't you come with me? Rabbits need not hide in burrows anymore; there won't be anything to be frightened of!"

"What? Leave my burrow and live in the open?" cried Stickle. "Not likely!" And he ran back home.

"But how do you *know* that rabbits will be safe there?" inquired Fickle.

"Because it says on this notice," said Christopher, "that the King will not allow anyone to hurt or destroy in all his land."

"I think I should like it there," said Fickle. "Tell me some more about it."

"It says the King will wipe away all tears and there will be no more death," said Christopher.

"But how do you know the notice is true?" asked Fickle.

"Because the King who wrote it cannot lie," replied Christopher.

"Then I'll go with you to this place," decided Fickle. So the two went on together.

"Come on," said Fickle impatiently, "let's waste no time in getting there."

"I can't go any faster," said Christopher. "This burden on my back slows me down."

As they went, talking together, suddenly they slipped and fell headlong into a great, miry swamp.

Christopher sank deeper and deeper into the mire, for his heavy burden weighed him down.

Fickle became angry. "What have you led me into?" he spluttered. "If this is what I have to go through to get to your Kingdom, then I'm not going!"

And he pulled himself out of the mire on the side nearest The Dark Wood and ran home.

Christopher struggled across the swamp to the side nearest the Narrow Gate. But however hard he tried, he could not get out. Then, just as he thought it was all over, help arrived.

On the bank appeared an old vole. He grinned at Christopher and held out his paw.

"Well now," he said, after setting Christopher on firm ground again. "What were you doing in the mire?"

"I'm going to The Evergreen Wood," explained Christopher. "The White Mouse directed me this way, when suddenly, I fell in."

"Why didn't you use the stepping-stones?" chuckled the Old Vole. And when Christopher looked, he could see the stones quite clearly.

"However did I miss them?" he wondered as he walked on toward the Narrow Gate.

CHAPTER 2
BADGER'S HOUSE

Christopher had not gone much farther before he came in sight of a fine-looking animal winding his way across the meadow toward him. The creature introduced himself as Mr. Townley Toad. He seemed a jolly sort, full of chat. Presently, he asked Christopher about the burden on his back.

"When I learned that The Dark Wood was to be destroyed," sighed the mouse, "it–it just grew, and no matter how hard I try, I cannot get it off."

"Oh, I know how you can get rid of that," proclaimed Mr. Townley Toad, puffing himself up a little.

"How? Tell me!" cried Christopher in great excitement.

"Just beyond this meadow lies a small grove," said Toad, waving his paw in that direction, "in the middle of which is an exceedingly tall pine tree . . ."

"Yes, go on," begged Christopher.

"At the very top of the Tall Pine Tree," continued the toad, "lives Beak, the tawny owl . . ."

When Toad said "owl" Christopher's mouth dropped wide open.

"He is excellent at taking off burdens," said Mr. Townley Toad, pushing Christopher off over the Meadow.

Christopher shuffled through the long, thick grass feeling dreadfully uneasy.

"What am I doing?" he thought miserably. "I have turned out of the way to make the acquaintance of an owl!" His knees shook, and his burden seemed even heavier. But it was because of his burden, and the hope of losing it, that Christopher continued on.

When at last he came upon the Tall Pine Tree, he hardly dared look up. And when eventually he did, his little body quaked with fear. For there, perching just above his head, was the owl. He looked huge and menacing, his talons mean and sharp. And as for his beak . . .

Christopher wished with all his heart that he was safely back on the path. And as he wished, a wonderful thing happened: White Mouse came scurrying through the trees toward him.

"Christopher," he panted. "You are in great danger! Come quickly back to the pathway."

"But I want to be rid of this burden," wept poor Christopher.

"No ordinary creature can rid you of that,"

explained White Mouse, hurrying Christopher to safety. "Now, go on, and do not leave the path. For although it *is* a difficult way, there is no danger there that you will not be able to conquer."

At last, Christopher reached the Narrow Gate. He tried hard to open it, but could not. Then he saw, carved upon it, these words:

KNOCK, AND IT SHALL BE OPENED

So Christopher knocked. Eventually the gate opened, and Christopher found himself being welcomed by Holgate Hedgehog.

"Hello, Mouse," he said, "and where might you be going?"

"Please, sir," said Christopher, "I am on my way to The Evergreen Wood."

A black shape suddenly swooped towards them, and Christopher felt a chill of cold air rush down upon him. Holgate grabbed him by the paw and quickly pulled him through the gate.

"What—what was that?" squeaked Christopher in alarm.

"Don't worry yourself," said Holgate, hastily shutting the gate again. "It's only them there crows. They forever watch this gate, waiting for creatures who dither about outside and for those who are too fearful to knock."

Christopher gulped.

"All alone are you?" inquired Holgate kindly.

"My wife and children were happy in The Dark Wood," said Christopher sadly. "They did not see the danger."

"Perhaps they'll be along later," encouraged the hedgehog.

"Yes, perhaps," said Christopher, wiping away a tear. "Fickle the rabbit accompanied me at the start, but when we fell into the mire, he decided to go home again."

"Dear me," wondered Holgate, "didn't he think it worth going through a few difficulties to reach The Evergreen Wood?"

Christopher inquired if it were possible to have his burden removed. But the hedgehog just shook his head and directed Christopher on his journey.

"Be sure you keep on the straight and narrow path," he warned, "and call in at Brockley Badger's house on your way. He'll have some interesting things to show you."

So Christopher trod on until he came to Brockley's house. He knocked hard upon the door, and the badger soon opened it, holding a candle in his paw.

"Come in, come in, Mouse," he said, "and rest yourself by the fire."

Brockley began to busy himself with his

sweeping brush. He liked a clean house, and Christopher had brought some dirt in on his shoes. But instead of the dust going out of the door, it flew into the air, getting in Christopher's eyes and throat and making him sneeze. "Kertyschoo!"

"Now, watch this," said Brockley, as he sprinkled a little water into the room. Immediately,

the dust cleared, and the badger was able to sweep it away quite easily.

"This dust is like our cares and worries," explained Brockley. "It chokes us and clouds our vision. But a little water will clear it all away." He offered a cup of it to Christopher. The mouse drank it and felt much better.

"Mmmm, it tastes good," he said.

"It *is* good," said Brockley earnestly. "This water was drawn from the Living Waters which flow directly from The Evergreen Wood. Whenever you drink it, you will find the help you need."

In one corner of the room, near to the warmth of the fire, hung a cage where a little dormouse lived.

"Why is Dormouse in a cage?" asked Christopher.

"Dormouse set off on the journey to The Evergreen Wood," explained Brockley, "but he was too fearful to continue, so I allow him to live here until he can find enough courage to go on."

Soon after, Christopher left, thanking Brockley for his kindness.

The path seemed to change now. There was a wall on either side, and Christopher felt curiously excited. He broke into a run. The path was leading upward, and at the top a white lamb stood waiting. In his hand he held a shepherd's staff. As Christopher came up to him, the burden on his back slipped off and rolled away.

"Welcome," said the Lamb. He

presented the mouse with a book, a key, and a new suit of clothes. Christopher's own clothes were very dirty from the mire.

"Read the Book," said the Lamb. "It will help you on your journey. And take care of the Key," he added, "for with it you will be able to unlock the gates of The Evergreen Wood."

So Christopher Mouse went on, without his burden and in his new suit of clothes, leaping for joy as he went.

CHAPTER 3
THE STEEP HILL

Christopher felt so happy, he sang a little song to himself:

> My burden's gone, now I'm free,
> New life has been given me,
> Strength to win the race ahead,
> Eyes to see where I should tread,
> Help to guide me through the day,
> Lest I stumble on the way.

Just as he had sung this, however, he very nearly fell upon three sleeping hares—

Loafer, Lounger, and Lazy-Bones—who were stretched out across the pathway. Their feet were shackled together with irons.

"Wake up!" cried Christopher urgently. "Why are you sleeping in the daytime?"

The three hares stirred.

"Why don't you ask the White Lamb to set you free?" continued the mouse.

"What lamb?" yawned Loafer.

"Just a little more rest," sighed Lounger.

"Let well enough alone," drawled Lazy-Bones. Then all three rolled over and fell asleep again. Christopher went on his way.

As he went, a pair of weasels came tumbling over the wall onto the pathway. Their names were Fiddle and Diddle, and Christopher learned that thcy, too, were going to The Evergreen Wood.

"Why did you climb over the wall," he questioned, "instead of entering in at the Narrow Gate?"

"Oh, that way is too far," said Fiddle, "so we took a short cut."

Christopher was concerned. "But it says in this Book," he explained,

"that there is only one way to reach The Evergreen Wood, and that is to keep upon the straight and narrow path."

Fiddle and Diddle looked at each other with a twinkle in their sharp little eyes. "Well, we're on it, aren't we?" they laughed.

Presently, they came to the foot of a very steep hill. Around it were two other pathways; one turned to the right and the other to the left. But the narrow way led straight up the hill.

Christopher kept his eyes on the way ahead and started up the hillside. But Fiddle and Diddle had no intention whatever of tiring themselves out by climbing the hill. They followed what they thought to be easier ways: one took the path to the right and the other the path to the left. They were never seen again.

After climbing halfway up the hill on his hands and knees, Christopher was at the point of exhaustion. So when he discovered a little mossy nest lying among a clump of marigolds, he eagerly climbed in to rest a while. He took out his Book and began to read, but his eyelids were heavy, and before long he fell into a deep sleep.

The sun sank low in the sky, and a chilly breeze blew over the hillside. Christopher woke with a start. "Oh, dear!" he moaned. "I didn't mean to fall asleep. I don't want to be left on this hillside in the dark." So he got up all in a rush and scrambled up the hill. When he reached the top, two field mice, named Quiver and Quake, came running down to meet him.

"What's the matter?" Christopher cried. "Why are you running the wrong way?"

"Ah, me!" squeaked Quiver. "The farther we go, the more danger we meet."

"What danger?" asked Christopher.

"Hawks!" squealed Quake. "Great hawks on the pathway! Just waiting!"

"We've had enough!" cried Quiver. "We're going home." And they ran back down the hill.

Christopher was beginning to panic. "Oh, what shall I do?" he asked himself. "I can't go back; The Dark Wood is to be destroyed. I *must* reach the safety of The Evergreen Wood." He felt in his pocket for his Book, that he might read some words of comfort, but it was missing!

"Oh, no!" he groaned in dismay. "How can I go on without my Book?"

Then he remembered falling asleep while reading it on the hillside. He ran back down the hill to the place where the marigolds grew and climbed again into the little nest where he had carelessly fallen asleep. And there, among the moss, lay his precious Book.

As he climbed back up the hill, he sighed to think that he had trod that path three times when he need only have trod it once.

"How far might I have been by now," complained Christopher, "if I had not spent the day sleeping!"

When he reached the top again, the moon had already risen. It was too dark to read now. He remembered the story that the field mice had told him, and shivered.

"What shall I do if I meet the hawks in the dark?" he thought gloomily. As he crept cautiously along, looking all about him, he came upon a great oak tree standing in a beautiful garden. A bright light shone down from a window at the top of the tree.

"I'll knock and ask if I can spend the night in the safety of the Garden," thought Christopher. But as he hurried toward the garden gate, he suddenly stopped, and his face grew pale. Ahead of him, sentinel-like by the gateposts, sat the hawks.

Christopher hesitated, and as he did, he heard a voice calling to him. "Fear not!" it said. "Keep to the middle of the path and no harm shall come to you."

Trembling from head to tail, the little mouse tiptoed along the path, making sure that he walked in the very centre of it. Keeping his eyes straight ahead and not daring even to look right or left, he crept past the hawks and reached the garden gate in safety.

"Well done!" said Mervin Mole, who kept watch by the garden gate. (It was he who had encouraged Christopher to go on.) "See, the birds are tethered," he chuckled. "They are only there to test your courage."

"Well I never!" Christopher said in amazement. "Who'd have thought it?" Then he asked Mervin if he might spend the night in the Garden.

"We'll see what the ladies have to say about that," said the mole, and he rang the bell which hung on the garden gate. A door opened at the foot of the Great Oak Tree, and a pretty red squirrel looked out. Her name was Beauty, and when she learned who Christopher was and where he was going, she ran and fetched her sisters: Ginger, Flame, and Honey.

The squirrels insisted that Christopher should be their guest and invited him to spend the night at the

top of the Great Oak Tree. Fortunately, there was a staircase inside; Christopher was not in the habit of climbing to the top of oak trees.

At the head of the stairs stood a stout oak door. Ginger flung it open, and the animals stepped into a snug little parlour. A log fire crackled merrily in the hearth, and over it hung a steaming cauldron of blackberry tea, while from the cinders beneath there arose the delicious smell of roasting chestnuts.

After a hearty meal, Christopher curled up on the parlour floor, near the warmth of the fire. The sweet oaken smell made him drowsy, and the trials of the day slipped away.

While he slept the squirrels set to work making some useful garments for his difficult journey ahead.

From the parlour window, the next morning, they showed Christopher the Cedar Grove. "When you reach the grove," Beauty said, "you will be able to see the gates of The Evergreen Wood."

Then they presented their gifts. "Dear Christopher," said Ginger, "please accept this breastplate. It will help protect you from the enemy that lies ahead."

"Wear this helmet," said Flame. "It will help save you from your enemy."

"With this shield," said Honey, "you will be able to fend off his fierce attacks."

"And this sword," said Beauty, "used with wisdom and courage, will bring you victory!"

When Christopher put the armour on, he suddenly *did* feel brave and full of courage for whatever dangers he might meet on the way ahead.

CHAPTER 4
THE BLACK VALLEY

Beauty, Ginger, Flame, and Honey accompanied Christopher down into the Black Valley on the other side of the hill. They kissed him goodbye and gave him some fresh acorns to eat on the way.

"Keep your sword in your hand," said Beauty. "Then you will be ready for whatever lies ahead."

And very soon, Christopher discovered just what did lie ahead, for sprawled out across the path, barring his way, lay a huge wild cat. His striped coat was torn and ragged, and one of his ears was missing. He got up and stretched himself when he saw Christopher approach.

"Where are you going, Mouse?" he drawled, surveying Christopher with his cold amber eyes.

"I–I'm going to The Evergreen W–Wood," stammered Christopher.

"Really?" said the cat, and the end of his tail twitched as if he were annoyed. "Do you know that this valley belongs to me and that I do not like creatures passing through my valley?"

"I–I didn't know," replied Christopher. "The p–path leads this w–way."

"The path also leads back to where you've come from," spat the Wild Cat, revealing his long, sharp fangs.

Christopher gripped his sword. "I–I'm not going back," he said boldly.

The cat cuffed him round the head, knocking him over. For a moment, Christopher thought of turning round and running back to the Great Oak Tree where the squirrels lived, but then he remembered that he did not have any armour on his back to protect him. He stood up, trying very hard to be brave. Then, taking courage, he lunged at the cat with his sword.

The cat leapt clear, screeching with anger, then turned and set upon the mouse, knocking the sword out of his hand.

Christopher fell to the ground, cut and bleeding. He almost gave up and wept pitifully. The cat was preparing to pounce again. Christopher roused himself just in time, and while crouching behind his shield managed to catch hold of his sword again. This time he held it in both paws and

lashed out desperately with all his might; it sliced through the air, cutting off the tip of the cat's tail.

The Wild Cat screamed out in pain and fury, then ran off at great speed across the valley. Christopher lay on the ground wounded and exhausted.

The Stream of Living Waters flowed through the valley, though its banks were overgrown with thorns and briars. Christopher hacked his way through and bathed his wounds in the cool water. He was healed immediately. He sat down, ate some of the acorns that the squirrels had given him, and thought. He thought about the dreadful fight with the Wild Cat and wondered at his own courage— courage which had enabled him to triumph over his enemy. He considered, too, that without the aid and assistance of Beauty, Ginger, Flame, and Honey, he would most certainly have had to turn back, for he would have stood no chance of victory against the Wild Cat without his armour.

Christopher hurried on. A blanket of thick, black clouds hung overhead, and the ground grew

soft and boggy. He tripped once or twice on clumps of deergrass that grew in the waterlogged valley. The pathway, at last leading to higher ground, had become a narrow ledge cut precariously into the rocky hillside.

He left his cumbersome sword and armour in the valley and stumbled into the gloom. Here and there the path had almost crumbled away, forcing him to hang on to tufts of white beak sedge and purple heather, which grew out of the rock, to save himself from slipping into the bog. Then he began to hear noises; strange, eerie sounds pierced the blackness. Fluttering, ghostly shapes in the air came within a whisker of him, then darted off again. Screams and screeches fell about him in a nightmare of terror.

Christopher crept into a cleft on the hillside and tried to hide. He lay there, trembling, striving to shut out the horrors of the Black Valley and wondering whether he had enough courage to go on.

How long he lay there he could not tell—perhaps hours. Eventually, the morning sun found a break in the clouds and chased the creatures of the night back to their shadowy hideouts.

The sunlight filled Christopher with new hope; he read some of the words in his Book until he felt

strong enough to go on. Then, as he stood up, he
heard a voice ahead of him singing:

Even though I walk alone,
Through Black Valleys far from home,
On this way I shall not fear,
Hardships soon will disappear,
And at last I shall be safe,
When I reach that wondrous place.

Christopher called out, "Hey, wait! Wait for
me!" and ran, as best he could without falling, until
he came upon the traveller. He was surprised to find
his countryman, Woodley Woodmouse.

"Why, Woodley!" Christopher shouted. "What
are you doing here?"

"Christopher!" cried Woodley in great
excitement. "I was hoping to meet you."

"But how did you get here?" asked Christopher.

"I left The Dark Wood soon after you. It–it
didn't seem the same, somehow, after you left,"
explained Woodley, and his soft brown eyes filled

with sorrow. "I–I knew you were right about leaving. It just took me a little longer to make up my mind."

Christopher smiled. "Well, you're ahead of me now, so you must have overtaken me at some time," he said. "Is there any news from home?"

"Yes, I have a letter for you," said Woodley, rummaging in his pocket. "Your wife, Christina, gave it to me before I left."

Christopher spread the crumpled letter out on the pathway and read eagerly:

> Dear Christopher,
>
> The children and I are very lonely without you. We are sorry now that we did not accompany you on your journey to The Evergreen Wood. But we are planning to set off ourselves, just as soon as we can. The White Mouse tells us that we have to wait for somebody called the Knight. I think he is some kind of trained guide.
> Anyway, the children are excited about it all and are looking forward to being together again – forever – as I am, dear husband.
>
> Yours,
> Christina

CHAPTER 5
RAT FAIR

At last the pathway left the evils of the Black Valley behind and led out onto common land. A colony of black rats lived in the land, and they had set up a fair there, with the intention of making a good living from the travellers passing by.

The mice looked around the stalls, hoping to find something useful for their journey. But they were sadly disappointed, shocked even, when they discovered just what the rats had for sale.

There were badges which read: "I've been to The Evergreen Wood."

"Buy a badge," grinned the stall-holder, "then you won't have to bother with the journey!"

Cheap imitations of the Books and Keys given

to Christopher and Woodley by the White Lamb
were for sale at exorbitantly high prices.

Whisker curlers, tail bows, and claw polish of
various colours were piled up on another stall.

There were charms which were supposed to
give protection from danger and cure-all potions
made from 'secret remedies'.

"You won't get in The Evergreen Wood without
a key, dearie," said the book and key stall-holder.

"I have a Key, thank you," said Christopher, "a
real one. And," he added, "I didn't have to buy it
either. It was given to me *free* by the White Lamb."

The rat scowled. "Don't you be clever with
me!" he said.

"Oh, look, Christopher!" exclaimed Woodley.
"Here are some maps for sale. I wonder whether
they have one of The Evergreen Wood."

"The Evergreen Wood?" mocked the stall-
holder. "Whatever do you want to go *there* for?
Look here, now here are some places *really* worth

going to." And he showed the mice some of his maps.

"There's Poison Ivy Wood—good food there," he said. "Or how about Eagles' Cove? Pretty there. Or there's the Black Valley. Nice quiet place that!"

Christopher and Woodley looked at each other in horror. "I know," said the rat, producing a dusty map from the bottom of the pile and brushing it off with his shirt sleeve. "The Dark Wood—nice place, full of potential!"

The mice slipped away, intending to cross the land as quickly as possible, but were detained when they came upon a poor little grey mouse whose feet were stuck fast in stocks.

"Why, Grey Mouse, who did this to you?"

asked Woodley. But Grey Mouse had wept so much
and had such a large lump in his throat
that he could not answer. Woodley
tried to lift the stocks to set the
creature free, but they were locked.

"Don't worry, Grey Mouse, I'll
get you out of there," he promised.

Grey Mouse could only squeak sadly.
Woodley strode off to have words with the Chief Rat.

"Why is Grey Mouse in the stocks?" he
demanded. "What harm has he done?"

"We don't like his type," sniffed the Chief.
"Thinks he's better than us. Accused us of cheating!
Little upstart!"

"Well you *are* cheats! Every one of you!"
retorted Woodley. "There is not one thing here
worth buying. Everything you have for sale
is useless!"

Woodley caused such a disturbance that all the
stall-holders gathered round to see what was going
on. The Chief Rat was shouting abuse at Woodley.

"Who do you think you are?" he yelled. "Aren't
we good enough for you?"

The stall-holders joined in with a chorus of
complaints. "Never bought a thing!" they jeered.
"Wasting our valuable time! Turned their noses up
at our good products!" they continued. "They need
a lesson or two. Yeah, show 'em what happens to
goody-goodies!"

Whereupon, Christopher and Woodley were arrested for disturbing the peace and were promptly locked in the stocks.

The little Grey Mouse, who was released to make room for the woodmice, scampered off home as fast as he could.

Christopher and Woodley had to bear the taunts and rebukes of the traders all afternoon. Some of them threw rotten crab apples and stale eggs, bruising the mice and spoiling their clothes.

Toward evening, when the stall-holders were busy packing away their wares, the Chief Rat unlocked the stocks and marched the mice across the land toward the hedgerow.

He pushed them down into a vast rat-hole underneath a blackthorn bush and pulled them through a long, dank burrow, until at last they stood in an open space, dimly lit and smelling strongly of ale.

Looking round, they saw they were in a sort of underground tavern. Several tables were littered about, and a number of black rats sat at them drinking beer. There was a sudden hush when the mice were brought in. The Bartender, a large rat wearing a brown apron, was leaning on the mantelpiece over a coal fire, warming his drink.

"Well, well, what have we here?" he said.

"These mice were disturbing the peace at Rat Fair," said the Chief Rat.

"What were you doing at the fair?" asked a skinny rat in the corner. He had his feet propped up on one of the benches and a keg of beer at his side.

"We–we thought we m–might b–buy something," stammered Christopher.

"But there was nothing worth buying!" claimed Woodley. This caused a great stir. Some of the rats stood on tables shouting. The fat rat in the apron banged his fist on the mantelpiece, spilling some of his spiced ale.

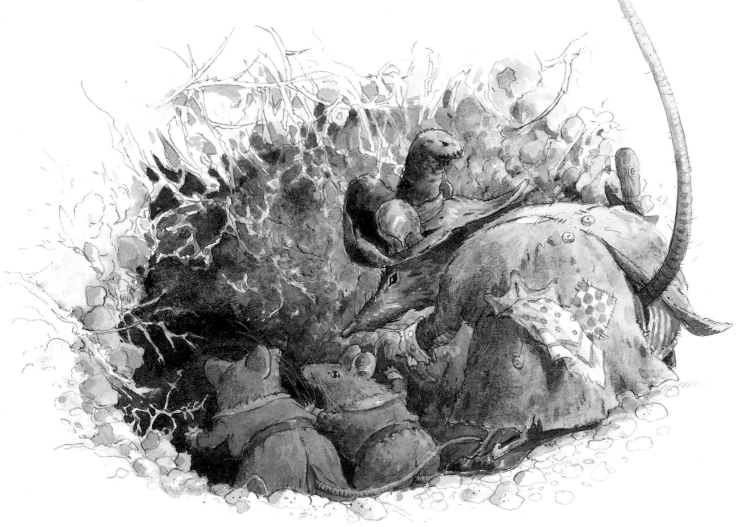

"Quiet!" he shouted. "The prisoners are obviously guilty. Pass the sentence, Chief."

The Chief Rat walked over to the fireplace and conferred with the Bartender. He took up a white-powdered wig which stood on one end of the mantelpiece and placed it on his head. He cleared his throat and pointed at Woodley, saying:

"I sentence you to six months hard labour— here in the Rat Hole. The Bartender will explain your duties."

And the Bartender, who had been busy writing out a long list, read out:

> 6:00 A.M. Light fire
>
> 7:00 A.M. Cook breakfast
>
> 8:00 A.M. Sweep floors
>
> 9:00 A.M. Scrub tables
>
> 10:00 A.M. Wash beer mugs

. . . and so the list went on.

"The other prisoner may be released," said the
Chief Rat.

Christopher clung to Woodley in despair.

"It's all right, Christopher. Time will soon
pass," said Woodley. "What are six months out of
eternity?"

Then Christopher was pushed out of the Rat
Hole, alone in the still night air.

A barn owl, ghostly white in the moonlight, flew
silently overhead, inspecting every blade of grass.

Christopher shivered. "I must get out of here
and find the path again," he thought as he crept
quietly along the hedgerow. Only when he came
within sight of the pathway did he feel safe enough
to stop and rest for the night. He found a bed of
wild strawberries and fell asleep beneath
the dark, crinkly leaves.

CHAPTER 6
FOX TERRITORY

Sunlight flickered through the strawberry leaves, rousing Christopher from his troubled dreams. He sat up and rubbed his eyes, and was on the point of selecting a bright red, juicy berry when he was disturbed by a rustle in the undergrowth. He was just wondering whether somebody else had plans to breakfast in the strawberry bed when a young black rat came hurrying through the hedgerow. He stopped when he saw Christopher.

"Good morning, sir. I'm Heathley," he said.

"Good morning, Heathley," said Christopher. "Would you like a strawberry?"

"N–no thank you," said the rat. "I'm not hungry. I–I'm going away, you know!"

Christopher looked surprised.

"I–I'm leaving this place—leaving it—and all its worthless ways forever!" The rat's voice was tight with emotion. "There are many more here, you know, who would like to get away, and they will one day, when they are ready. Please, sir," he begged, "may I accompany you on your journey to The Evergreen Wood?"

Christopher, of course, was delighted, and the

two creatures went on together. Before long they found themselves in a peaceful glade, full of lilies. The Stream of Living Waters flowed through the Glade, and along its banks grew green trees that bore every type of fruit that was good to eat.

Christopher and Heathley stayed in the Glade for several days, just eating and sleeping. They sang:

> In green meadows let us lie,
> With still waters flowing by,
> From fruitful trees let us eat
> 'fore we lie again to sleep.

When they had finished resting, they filled their pockets with apples and hazelnuts and followed the path out of the Glade. But the sweetness of that place was soon forgotten, for the way ahead became hard and difficult. Rough stones littered the path, making their feet sore and their hearts heavy.

Presently, however, they came to some steps, and beyond them they could see a pleasant meadow with a grassy path winding through it.

"Heathley," cried Christopher, "let us go over the steps and follow the path through the meadow."

"But suppose it leads us out of the way?" said Heathley in a worried voice.

"That's not likely," said Christopher, "for it is just the other side of the hedge, and I believe it will soon meet up again with our own pathway."

So Heathley was persuaded and followed Christopher over the steps.

A little later, they came upon another traveller wandering along the soft, grassy pathway. His name was Falter Frog, and Christopher asked him if he knew where the path led.

"To The Evergreen Wood," replied the frog.

"There, Heathley, I told you so!" said Christopher.

They followed Falter until nightfall. Then it began to rain. Christopher looked up at the sky; black clouds swirled overhead. "A storm is brewing," he said, pulling his coat collar up round his chin. "We must find some shelter." There was a great clap of thunder, and then the rain poured down in torrents. The ditch that ran alongside the path was filled to overflowing with muddy rainwater and was threatening to spill over and flood the pathway at any moment.

Suddenly, there was a splash, and Falter Frog disappeared.

"Falter, are you all right?" called Christopher.

There was an answering "Croak! Croak!" and that was the last they ever heard of Falter.

"It's all very well for him," complained Christopher. "He can spend the night in the ditch; we can't!"

"I wonder where we are," said Heathley, as a flash of lightning lit up the flooded meadow.

Christopher began to feel uneasy. "Oh, dear!" he groaned. "I think we might be lost!"

"I thought we went the wrong way," sighed Heathley, as the ditch water finally burst its banks and lapped round his knees.

"We must get back to the steps," cried Christopher urgently.

But the flood water was getting deeper and deeper, and they were in danger of being washed away. Christopher felt the water swirl around his legs and drag at his body. He stumbled, and as he did, he reached out and caught hold of some ivy leaves that were floating down from an old willow stump. Heathley had managed to do the same, and together they climbed the ivy and pulled themselves up onto the flat top of the Old Willow. They lay down, exhausted, beneath the canopy of glossy green ivy leaves and fell fast asleep.

Not far from where they slept, a fox's lair lay hidden in the shrub of a juniper wood. The Fox had been out all night inspecting his land, and on his way home in the morning, he saw Christopher and Heathley asleep on the tree stump.

"Wake up!" he barked. "What are you doing on my land?"

Christopher and Heathley awoke with a start.

"We–we lost our way," squeaked Christopher.

"You are trespassers!" growled the Fox. "And trespassers must be prosecuted!"

Whereupon, he caught hold of Christopher and Heathley by the backs of their necks and carried them off to his lair. He pushed them inside his dingy, dark earth, then lay down by the entrance and went to sleep.

"Oh, dear!" wailed Christopher. "Whatever shall we do?"

"Come, my friend," said Heathley, "I have some ivy berries and one or two hazelnuts in my pocket. We will feel better it we eat something."

"I couldn't eat a thing," wept Christopher.

"It's all my fault: trying to find an easier way! Now we're doomed!"

"We must think of a plan," said Heathley, ignoring his friend's outburst. "Maybe we could creep past the Fox while he sleeps?"

Together they tiptoed nearer and nearer the entrance.

Then suddenly, the Fox opened his huge jaws and yawned. At the sight of so many long, sharp teeth—some of them stained with blood—the little friends ran back and hid in the darkest corner of the burrow.

"Oh! Oh! Oh!" cried Christopher. "We shall never get out of here!"

"Please, Christopher, don't give up," begged Heathley. "Remember how you escaped from the tawny owl and the Wild Cat? Well, we can escape from this dark dungeon if we only try!"

The rat sat down and thought. And as he thought, he began to paw at the soft earth of the Fox's burrow. Suddenly, he jumped up, squealing.

"What is it?" cried Christopher.

"See how soft this earth is!" exclaimed Heathley, beginning to dig furiously in the side of the burrow. "We'll dig our way out!"

Christopher ran to help him, scraping and scratching at the earth with all his might.

"Dig upwards," ordered Heathley, scooping out the soil with his powerful back legs.

Before long, a chink of light appeared at the end of the tunnel. Then the sunlight flooded in upon them, and they stood, free at last, in the sweet green Juniper Wood.

CHAPTER 7
THE EVERGREEN WOOD

Christopher and Heathley did not stop running until they reached the safety of the pathway on the other side of the steps.

"I shall leave a notice on the steps," said Christopher, "to prevent others from following that way." He wrote:

O'er these steps the way looks fair,
But, dear travellers, please take care,

For evil and dark despair,
Lurk within a Fox's lair.

Many creatures *did* read the notice and so escaped that terrible danger.

The path led the mice into an ancient cedar grove. The great trees spread their massive limbs out over the grove, as if in tender sympathy with the creatures that walked beneath them. A flock of turtle-doves had made its home among the thick, green foliage. One of them flew down and spoke to Christopher and Heathley.

"Good day," she cooed. "Welcome to the Cedar Grove."

"Good day," replied Heathley. "I wonder whether you could tell us how far it is to The Evergreen Wood?"

"Too far for any but those that shall reach it," answered the Turtle-dove.

"Is the way safe or dangerous?" inquired Heathley.

"Safe for those for whom it is to be safe," replied the dove.

She flew up onto a wide, drooping branch. "If you would like to climb up here," she called, "you may see the very gates of that wood."

Christopher and Heathley scrambled up onto

the broad bough and peered into the distance.

Christopher's eyes grew wide. "Can you see them?" he asked the rat.

"I—I think I can," said Heathley, peering through the trees.

Before they left the Cedar Grove, the Turtle-dove presented them with directions of the way. "Beware of false friends," she warned. "And take care that you do not sleep upon the Enchanted Ground."

Then she flew away, and Heathley tucked the map in his inside coat pocket.

And so, much encouraged, the two creatures set off, hoping that it would not be long before they reached the Gateway that would lead them into The Evergreen Wood.

Soon after, a little crooked lane met the pathway, and wandering along it, looking this way and that, came Shady the water shrew. Christopher asked him where he came from.

"I live in the Marsh at the bottom of the Little Crooked Lane," he said. "But I'm on my way to The Evergreen Wood."

"How are you going to get in without a Key?" asked Christopher.

Shady thought for a moment. "Oh, I expect I shall find a way," he said carelessly. He broke off every now and then to take a dip in the ditch that was by the wayside, so Christopher and Heathley soon overtook him.

Presently, the path divided, and as they paused to consider which way to go, a grey rabbit came hopping toward them.

"Follow me," he called over his shoulder. "This is the way."

They followed the Grey Rabbit for some time. Then suddenly the ground beneath their feet gave way, and they found themselves falling.

Down and down they fell, until at last they came to the bottom of an enormous rabbit hole.

"Oow!" squealed Christopher as he hit the earth with a thump. "What are we going to do now?"

"Ooh!" Heathley wailed, as he came tumbling down beside him. "We should have paid more attention to the Turtle-dove. She warned us to beware of false friends."

"And we forgot to read the map she gave us!" groaned Christopher. They lay there, sad and lonely, at the bottom of the hole for some time.

Eventually, the sound of tiny feet could be heard far above them. Somebody called , "Christopher! Heathley!" and a pale, anxious face peered down.

"It's the White Mouse!" cried Christopher, jumping up and down in excitement. "Oh, White Mouse," he shouted, "how pleased I am to see you!"

The White Mouse, in anticipation of such a problem, had brought with him a long rope. He wrapped one end of this around a tall ash tree; the other end he lowered over the edge of the deep hole. "Catch hold of the rope," he called, "and pull yourselves up."

When they were once again standing on firm ground, Christopher hugged the White Mouse. "Thank you for rescuing us," he cried.

"And we're sorry," sighed Heathley, "for causing you so much trouble."

"You would cause me a lot less trouble," said the White Mouse sternly, "if you would only follow your instructions! Now, let me guide you back to the pathway."

The sorry pair trudged behind, with their heads bowed to the ground. When they reached the pathway, the sun had already gone down, and the stars were shining brightly in the sky. The White Mouse made a bed of dry leaves under the roots of a wide beech tree.

"We'll rest here for the night," he said. Heathley gathered some of the beechnuts that lay all about, and they sat cracking the shells in the moonlight and nibbling on the little seeds inside.

Christopher and Heathley awoke the next morning to find that the White Mouse had already gone. They continued their journey uneventfully for much of the day. Then the path led them into a wooded valley. Heathley sniffed the air; it was heavy with the sweet scent of honeysuckle and bluebells. The sun flickered warmly on their heads, and flying insects hummed and droned lazily about them. The rat yawned.

"Ah, let us lie down and take a nap," he said wearily. "I can hardly keep my eyes open."

"Oh, no!" said Christopher urgently. "If we fall

asleep here, we may never wake up again! For we are walking upon the Enchanted Ground!"

"Oh, dear!" cried Heathley. "If I had been here alone, I would have been in great danger!"

"Well, two are better than one," said Christopher. And he sang a song to keep them awake:

> Be alert, stay wide awake,
> Keep on going, don't hesitate.
> On this ground enchantments lie,
> Slumbering valleys heave and sigh,
> Calling creatures to the deep
> Unfathomed depths of silent sleep.

Having safely passed over the Enchanted Ground, they rested for a while beside a lily pond. Here they met the little water shrew again, basking in the sunny waters.

The three went on together until they came within sight of the Gateway. Christopher and Heathley gazed in wonder. But as they drew nearer, they saw to their dismay that a very deep and wide river lay between them and the Gateway.

They looked for a bridge to go over, but there was none.

"We shall have to swim across," said Heathley, discarding his shoes on the river bank.

"Do you think we shall make it?" asked Christopher in a very squeaky voice.

"If we do not panic," said the rat, "we should manage quite easily."

Christopher entered the water with some trepidation. He and Heathley swam side by side. All went well at first, but towards midstream the current became stronger, and Christopher Mouse grew anxious.

"Oh, Heathley," he cried out, "I shall be swept away!"

"Keep going, Christopher; we have almost reached the other side!" encouraged Heathley.

But Christopher began to panic. "I don't think I can make it," he spluttered, as a wave washed over his ears.

"You *can* make it—you *can*!" insisted Heathley. And he stretched out his paw and held his friend's head above water until they reached the bank on the other side.

Meanwhile, Shady had been nosing about in the water reeds and had discovered an old flat-bottomed boat. Shady loved boats. He leapt onto it, poled it free of the reeds, and glided off down the river. Christopher and Heathley saw him go. Shady seemed to have forgotten all about them and The Evergreen Wood.

Christopher took the Key out of his inside coat pocket and turned the lock.

The gates swung open. Bright sunlight beamed down upon them and glowed through the tall, green trees. The Stream of Living Waters sparkled wide and fresh through the wood, and golden flowers grew along its banks.

Christopher breathed in the clean, sweet air and felt the peace and security all around him.

A great company of animals stood waiting to greet them. They cried:

"Welcome to The Evergreen Wood!" and "Well done, you faithful creatures! Come and share our happiness!"

They crowded round the heroes, each wanting

to greet them with a brotherly kiss.

Their own White Mouse was there too. "Come, we have prepared a feast for you," he said. "I have some good news, too," he added. "Woodley has been released and is on his way!"

"Hooray!" shouted Christopher and Heathley.

"And," said White Mouse, "the Knight will be arriving soon with Christina and the children!"

"My happiness," said Christopher, "is almost complete."

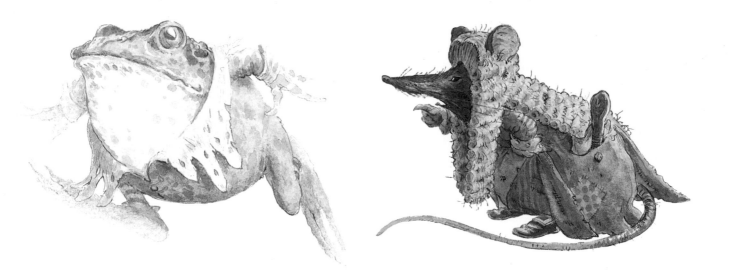